TM & copyright © by Dr. Seuss Enterprises, L.P. 2022

All rights reserved. Published in the United States by Random House Children's Books,
a division of Penguin Random House LLC, New York. The artwork that appears herein was
adapted from *The Cat in the Hat,* TM & copyright © 1957, and copyright renewed 1985 by
Dr. Seuss Enterprises, L.P., and *The Cat in the Hat Comes Back,* TM & copyright © 1958,
and copyright renewed 1986 by Dr. Seuss Enterprises, L.P.

Random House and the colophon and Beginner Books and colophon are registered trademarks of
Penguin Random House LLC. The Cat in the Hat logo ® and © Dr. Seuss Enterprises, L.P. 1957,
renewed 1986. All rights reserved.

Visit us on the Web!
Seussville.com
rhcbooks.com

Educators and librarians, for a variety of teaching tools, visit us at RHTeachersLibrarians.com

Library of Congress Cataloging-in-Publication Data is available upon request.
ISBN 978-0-593-43128-3 (trade) — ISBN 978-0-593-43129-0 (lib. bdg.)

MANUFACTURED IN CHINA
10 9 8 7 6 5 4 3 2 1
First Edition

IF I WERE SAINT NICK

A CHRISTMAS STORY

by **the Cat in the Hat**
with a little help from **Alastair Heim**

illustrated by **Tom Brannon**

BEGINNER BOOKS®
A Division of Random House

A letter just came
from the BIG MAN IN RED.
He sent it to ME!
Oh, the things that he said. . . .

He wrote me to say

that he wanted to know

if I would take charge

of the WHOLE NORTH POLE SHOW

if ever he needed

a break or a pause—

to rest or relax

(or perhaps . . . just BE-CLAUS)!

If I were Saint Nick,
oh, what fun it would be!
Just THINK of what Christmas
would be like with ME. . . .

If I were Saint Nick
and the North Pole were mine,
Thing One and Thing Two
would wrap line after line
of TWINKLE-ISH tinsel
around every tree
and cover the buildings
in twinkly glee . . .

. . . to make the most TINSEL-ISH
sight you could see!

If I were Saint Nick,
I would make a NEW list.
Not NAUGHTY or NICE.
No, a list with a TWIST!
My LIST WITH A TWIST
would be made up of names
of the boys and the girls
who like mess-making games.

NAUGHTY

BLAKE
JOSÉ
PAT
SAM

ZAR
CHRI
JI

SUE
ALEX
KAI
NALA

Do YOU think your name
should be on my list?
I always check TWICE
so that no one is missed!

If I were Saint Nick,
we would read all your letters
before we change into
our TOY-MAKING sweaters.

Dear Saint Nick,

Please bring me a
red trike. Sally

Saint Nick
North Pole

The letters you send
help my elves do their best
to make all the toys
that your letters request. . . .

A TOY-MAKING sweater
has tricks up its sleeve,
and gizmos and gadgets
you WOULD NOT believe,
to make all the presents
that you will receive
(when I bring them by
to your house Christmas Eve)!

If I were Saint Nick,
we would use giant cranes
to haul all these
tall
   tall
      tall
         tall
candy canes.

The CANE CRANES would lift them
and haul up them all . . .
which helps when your stockings
are FOUR STORIES tall!

If I were Saint Nick,
we would wrap every present
in CAROLING PAPER
that sounds oh so pleasant.

Just give every box a big
SHAKE, SHAKE, SHAKE, SHAKE!
The more that you shake,
the more music they make!

If I were Saint Nick,
I would count down from TEN,
then skip right to FOUR,
then to ZERO, and then . . .

. . . my sleigh would go WHOOSH
as I fly oh so high
and do LOOP THE LOOPS
through the winter-y sky!

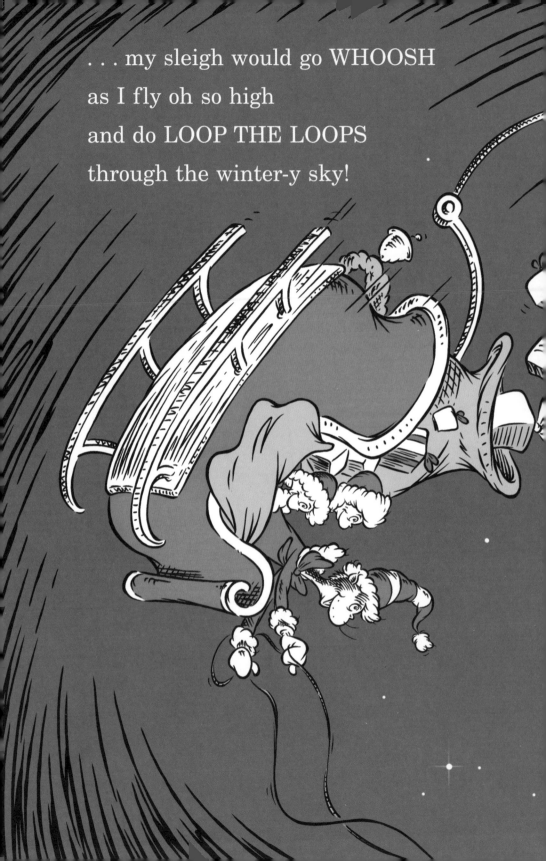

If I were Saint Nick,
I would cover your roof
with snow I would blow
from my SOUNDPROOFING-SNOOF....

The snow from the SNOOF
would drop with a PLOP
and quiet the sound
as we slide to a STOP.
(To keep you asleep
when we land up on top!)

If I were Saint Nick,
I would tiptoe around,
and walk extra softly
to not make a sound,
and check to be sure
you were snug in your bed,
then bid you good night
with a pat on your head.

If I were Saint Nick,
I would wear a NEW suit,
with plenty of pockets
and pouches, to boot,
to store all the snacks
and the goodies you make,
and cookies for Santa
that all of you bake.

If I were Saint Nick,
I would stand by your tree.
Thing One and Thing Two
would be right there with me . . .

. . . to pile your presents
on tables and chairs!
And stack them on shelves
and in pairs on the stairs!

FROM: THE FISH

The gifts I would give
would be FUN as can be.
So, if you get SOCKS,
they did NOT come from me!

Then, high in the sky
at the end of the night,
I would say to you all
as I drove out of sight . . .

"Your presents are waiting!
My work here is done!
Merry Christmas to all
and to all some GOOD FUN!"

And, when I was through,
I would kick up my feet
(and sit in the tub
with a big cake to eat)
and think of the smiles
and JOLLY GOOD cheer
that WE got to bring
to your Christmas this year.

If I were Saint Nick,
it would be oh so good!
If HE were to need me . . .

. . . do YOU think I should?